The GRAMMAR'S SLAMMIN' Muscle-Bound Compounds

By: Pamela Hall
Illustrated by: Gary Currant

magic wagon

visit us at www.abdopublishing.com

Published by Magic Wagon, a division of the ABDO Group, 8000 West 78th Street, Edina, Minnesota 55439. Copyright © 2009 by Abdo Consulting Group, Inc. International copyrights reserved in all countries. All rights reserved. No part of this book may be reproduced in any form without written permission from the publisher.

Looking Glass Library™ is a trademark and logo of Magic Wagon.

Printed in the United States.

Text by Pamela Hall
Illustrations by Gary Currant
Edited by Stephanie Hedlund and Rochelle Baltzer
Interior layout and design by Neil Klinepier
Cover design by Neil Klinepier

Library of Congress Cataloging-in-Publication Data
Hall, Pamela.
 The muscle-bound compounds / by Pamela Hall ; illustrated by Gary Currant.
    p. cm. -- (Grammar's slammin')
 Includes bibliographical references.
 ISBN 978-1-60270-616-3
 1. English language--Compound words--Juvenile literature. I. Currant, Gary, ill. II. Title.
 PE1175.H37 2009
 428.1--dc22
                                    2008036328

"I'm a walking, sloshing mess," Tea complained.
"I'm pretty splintered, too," Board muttered.
"Let's hit the gym."

3

Inside, the buff trainer, Link, rushed over.

"Welcome to Fitness Connection," he said. "It looks like you two could use a Compound Word Workout. We'll match you with other words to make you stronger and more useful."

Tea and Board looked around the gym. They watched Pony snare Bow to lift weights. But the barbell shifted for this lopsided pair.

"Whoa, slow down," Link sputtered. "*Ponybow* is not a word, you know. Let's get you two new Compound Connections."

"Look!" Pony exclaimed with pride. "We've combined to make *Ponytail*. It's a word with its own meaning. Now we can be three things—a Pony, a Tail, and a Ponytail."

But no one was listening! They were too busy
watching Rain and Bow combine to make a Rainbow.

Now all the words wanted to find their best match.

"I want a word to kick me up a notch," buzzed Fly. "Everyone swats at me!"

Link motioned to Dragon, who was stumbling over everybody. "You two will hit it off big," Link guessed.

Dragon and Fly joined
on the racquetball court.
The balls flew and *voilà!*
"Cool," sang Dragonfly.
"I'm a better bug and
Dragon can still fly—but at
a smaller size!"

Link spent that whole day working with words to increase muscle mass and meaning. Each new pair created a compound word.

Lace wanted an edgier look. So, she paired up with Shoe and together they made Shoelace. After that, they were tied up all day in an aerobics class.

Stop said to Watch, "You and I will keep great time as Stopwatch. And you won't have to work round the clock!"

Next, Note and Book joined together. They soon had a Notebook filled with race times that Stopwatch shouted to them.

Even Whirl slowed down long enough to splash around with Pool. Suddenly all the compound words were relaxing their muscles in the Whirlpool.

Lifeguard On Duty

Only Tea and Board weren't in the Whirlpool. Neither one of them were members of a compound team.

Cup tipped over to Tea. Tea poured himself inside.
"Aah, that feels good," Cup said. "We brewed up a
Teacup!"

"What do you say, Board?" asked Link.

Board was amazed! He had found his match with Cup as well.

"Now when Teacup needs a place to sleep," bragged Cupboard, "she can come our way. Cupboard is always open!"

"That's good," sighed Link, "because we have more words to beef up! You might find more compound words on your shelves than just Teacup."